NIU Press is pleased to work with the P-20 Center at Northern Illinois University to publish a series of STEM-based storybooks for young readers.

The P-20 Center collaborates with university and community partners to promote innovation in teaching and learning, and foster educational success for all ages.

The Stuffed Bunny Science Adventure Series for young readers is an extension of STEM Read, a P-20 program that helps readers explore the science, technology, engineering, and math concepts behind popular fiction.

This series shares the adventures of a fluff-brained bunny named Bear and his favorite boy, Jack. In each story, Bear meets other toys who teach him about the world around him. The books explore the importance of working together and making friends. They also incorporate STEM concepts aligned with the Next Generation Science Standards. Learn more about the Stuffed Bunny Science Adventure Series and find resources, videos, and games at stemread.com.

Northern Illinois University Press, DeKalb 60115

25 24 23 22 21 20 19 18 17 16   1 2 3 4 5

978-0-87580-742-3 (cloth)

978-1-60909-202-3 (ebook)

Library of Congress Cataloging-in-Publication Data

is available online at http://catalog.loc.gov

Printed in South Korea

Production Date March 2016

Plant & Location Printed by We SP Corporation (Gyunggi-do, Korea)

Job/Batch # 6632-0

The Toy and the TIDE POOL

A Stuffed Bunny Science Adventure

By Gillian King-Cargile
Illustrations by Kevin Krull

NORTHERN ILLINOIS UNIVERSITY PRESS

One salty, sandy day, a stuffed bunny named Bear sat at the beach playing pirates with his favorite boy, Jack. The big blue ocean lay in front of them. Seagulls cawed and circled overhead as the bunny and his boy searched for shiny treasure in the wet sand.

Reading at the

"Bear!" Jack yelled. "X marks the spot for hungry!" Jack pulled a bag of potato chips out of his family's picnic basket.

The boy was good at sharing. "One for me. One for Bear." He made a pile of potato chips on Bear's lap. "Two for me. Two for Bear." The crumbly chip pile got bigger and bigger, and Bear's fluffy tummy rumbled.

"Yum!" Bear said. "I love pretend-eating potato chips!" But around Bear and his boy the sky grew dark with bird-shaped shadows.

Hungry seagulls screeched and swooped at the potato chips. "I'm Pirate Jack, and this is *our* snack!" Jack yelled.

"Arr!" Bear shouted in his bravest pirate voice. "Go away, gulls!" But the birds didn't seem to understand Toy.

The biggest seagull of all snatched Bear up in its beak.

"Bear!" Jack yelled. "Come back!"

Down the shore, the bird flipped Bear back and forth.

When his fluff brain was very rattled and the chips were all shaken loose, the seagull opened his beak and let Bear fall.

He flopped down on a wet and rocky shore.
"Oh no," Bear said sadly. "Alone again!"

"You're not alone," a Toy voice called out. "This tide pool is filled with life!" Bear saw a mermaid doll flapping her tail and making ripples in a deep puddle of water that was cut off from the ocean by rocks.

"I am Princess Shelleena from the kingdom of the Mer Magic Underwater Enchantment Play Set." Bear had played princesses with Jack's sister Sophie before, so he knew it was proper to bow to royal ladies.

"I am Bear," he said. "From the kingdom of Jack's house. Did you get carried off by a seagull too?"

Princess Shelleena shook her head. The sun sparkled off her tiara. "My girl and I were playing in the ocean. A strong wave knocked me out of her hands. I washed up here and got knotted in this dirty old net." Princess Shelleena smiled at Bear. "Perhaps you can rescue me?"

Bear hopped over and tried to free Princess Shelleena. "Sorry," Bear said. "My paws are too squishy to untangle knots, and my claws are just sewed-on thread. I'm just too fluff-brained to rescue anybody."

"Blasted barnacles!" Princess Shelleena huffed. "If only I had the nail file from my Mer Magic Manicure set. I could have cut my way out of this net nineteen high tides ago. A proper princess should always be prepared."

Princess Shelleena returned her gaze to the deep puddle between the rocks.

Bear peered in the water too. This wasn't like the muddy puddles he and Jack splashed in after storms. "At least we're stranded by a very nice puddle," Bear said.

"This isn't a puddle, Sir Bear. It's a tide pool. Water is left here when the tide goes out. This pool is full of amazing animals." Princess Shelleena told Bear to sit very still and watch the water.

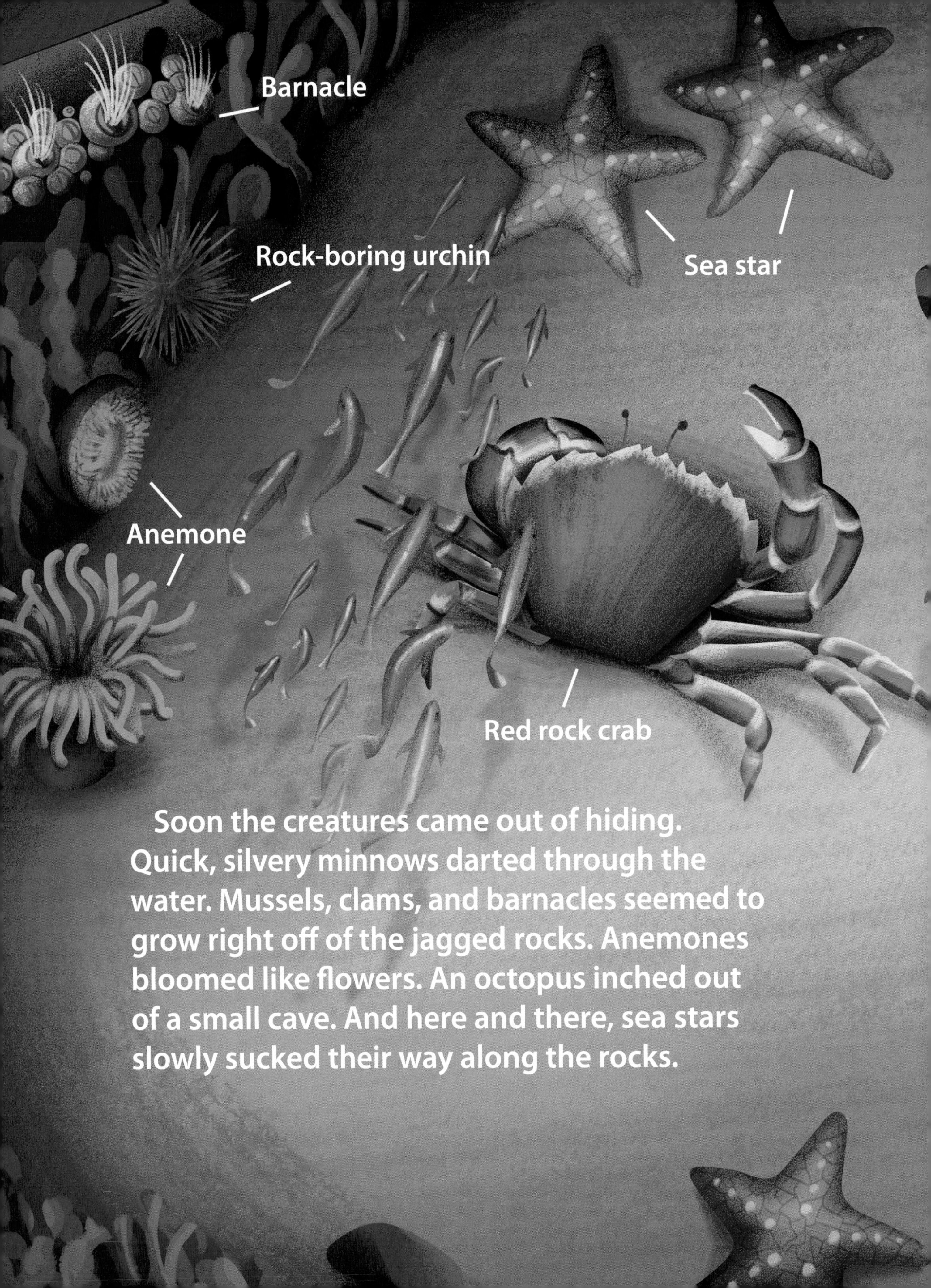

Soon the creatures came out of hiding. Quick, silvery minnows darted through the water. Mussels, clams, and barnacles seemed to grow right off of the jagged rocks. Anemones bloomed like flowers. An octopus inched out of a small cave. And here and there, sea stars slowly sucked their way along the rocks.

“These are some of the hardiest creatures in the ocean,” Princess Shelleena said. “They have to adjust to changing water levels, changing temperatures, and rough waves. And those terrible seagulls are always trying to eat them.”

“It’s beautiful,” said Bear. “Except for the seagulls.”

"Beautiful, but temporary," Princess Shelleena said. "Right now, you're trapped here like me and my ocean friends, but even now the water rises."

"Twice a day, the high tide comes, flooding the rocky shore and overflowing the tide pools. Twice a day, my new friends are washed away into deeper water while I stay stuck."

"I can't get sucked out into the ocean," Bear yelled. "My fluffy stuffing will fill with water!"

"Sir Bear, don't give up." Princess Shelleena patted Bear's paw and shook her sparkly-crowned head. "If you believe you are a little more brave or a little less fluff-brained, we can think of a way out of this."

A wave surged over the rocks, filling the tide pool higher. Bear backed away, but the water licked at his fabric feet.

Just then, Bear heard a voice calling over the
crashing of the waves. "Bear," the voice yelled. . .
WHERE ARE YOU?

"Jack!" Bear yelled, but his Toy voice was too tiny for Jack and his family to hear. "I have to get their attention."

“If only I had my Mer Magic Wand,” Princess Shelleena sighed. “It always shines bright in the darkest waters.”

“That’s it!” Bear said. “I need something shiny!” He grabbed Princess Shelleena’s tiara and held it so that it reflected the fading sun.

Down the beach, Jack's family was about to give up the search.

"Wait," Jack shouted. "Something shiny over in those rocks!"

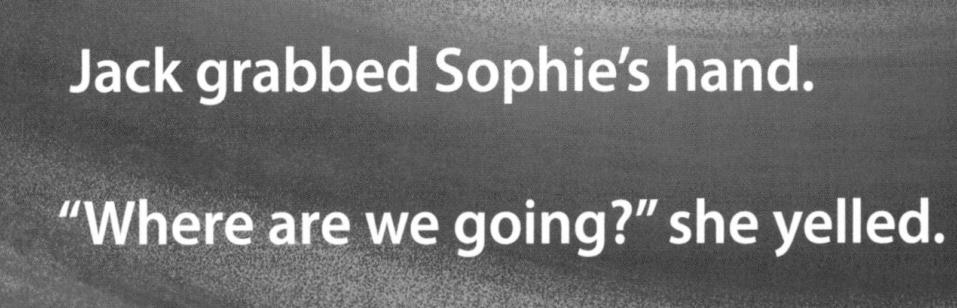

Jack grabbed Sophie's hand.

"Where are we going?" she yelled.

"To find pirate treasure!"

"Bear!" Jack yelled. "You did find treasure!"

Sophie saw the mermaid. "It's a Princess Shelleena doll!" Sophie pulled a multi-tool out of her waist pack and freed the princess from the net.

"Would you like to come home with me?"

Princess Shelleena smiled at Bear. "What did I tell you, Sir Bear? Proper princesses are always prepared!"

Jack hugged the water out of Bear's soggy fabric fluff. "You battled a bird and saved a mermaid," Jack said. "You're the bravest bunny ever!"

Bear had had enough bravery for one day. He was happy to be back with his boy. The toys and their children set off down the beach in search of dry clothes, warm dinner, and another exciting adventure.

George Parsons,
Shedd Aquarium's Senior Director of Fishes

Ever wonder where sea turtles swim or how long whales can hold their breath? Do you love to swim and spend time by the water? Maybe you should be a marine biologist!

What is a marine biologist?

Marine biologists are scientists who study plants and animals that live in and around the world's oceans. They work everywhere from laboratories and offices to ships and oil rigs. They even work underwater, scuba diving and riding in submarines.

What is a tide pool?

A tide pool is a puddle left by regular sea-level changes called tides. Sea life can get trapped in these pools at low tide and must wait for high tide to get back out to sea. Some animals live in tide pools and rely on them to find food. Tide pools hold amazing ocean creatures close to shore so we can appreciate them without getting wet!

What causes high and low tides?

Tides are caused by our moon, the sun, and the rotation of our planet. As the earth spins, different parts of its oceans pass closer to the moon. When an area of the ocean is close to the moon, the water is drawn up toward it, creating a high spot, which we call "high tide." If you stood on the beach all day, you would notice that the water is higher or lower depending on the tide. Most places have two high and two low tides a day.

Why do creatures need to be hardy to live in tide pools?

Tide pools often form in eroded rocks, which can be sharp and dangerous. They also change temperature as the sun heats their shallow water. Creatures have adapted to life in this environment. Many have special ways to cling to rocks so they don't get smashed or cut. When water disappears, they can hold on to moisture until the next wave or tide.

What are some dos and don'ts for visiting tide pools?

- **Do** make sure people know where you are going. Go with a guide or adult.
- **Do** check a tide schedule so you know the cycle. Always be aware of the time and your surroundings. The ocean can change very quickly. If you are unsure of an area, stay very close to shore. You'll see just as many critters.

- **Do** wear very sturdy shoes that can get wet, such as canvas tennis shoes. They help you get traction and protect your feet from slippery, sharp rocks.
- **Don't** touch animals you don't know, for their safety and yours! Tide pool animals are wild. Some pinch. Some are venomous. Some are even toxic.
- **Don't** poke animals or pry them off rocks. Most tide pool creatures are sturdy but fragile. Removing them from the tide pool could hurt or kill them.

What are some of the coolest tide pool creatures?

Anemones close up at low tide. At high tide, they open into flower-like animals. Their beautiful arms have toxic stinging cells that help them hunt fish.

Octopi can squeeze into tiny spaces that are just slightly bigger than their beaks. They can also scuttle across dry rocks to find food, another tide pool, or deeper water.

Clingfish use their fins to form a strong suction cup that holds them to rocks when strong waves or currents enter the tide pool.

Sea stars are star-shaped predators. They can pry open a clam and then push their stomachs out of their bodies to digest the clam inside its own shell.

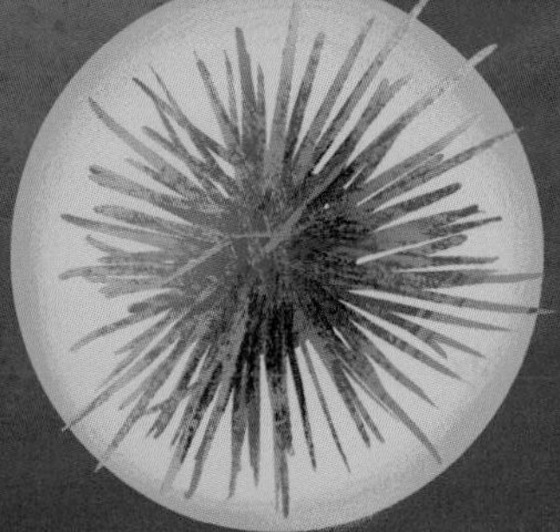

Rock-boring urchins are round, super-spiny animals that are a cousin of sea stars. They gnaw all day on limestone, creating grooves that help them catch water to stay wet and to grow their own food: algae. They also create sand as they poop out bits of rock.

What should readers do if they want to become marine biologists?

Talk to your teacher! Growing up in Illinois, I asked my fifth-grade science teacher how I could learn about the ocean. He set up an aquarium so we could study ocean creatures up close. He and other teachers helped me decide to become a marine biologist and a curator at a public aquarium. I studied science (mostly biology) and math. I visited and volunteered at aquariums and zoos. I got comfortable boating, swimming, and scuba diving. Every chance I got, I would spend time near oceans and lakes to observe and explore. Tide pools have always been a source of inspiration for me!

Find more Stuffed Bunny Science Adventure resources, videos, and games at stemread.com.